The Sesame Seed Snatchers

The Sesame Seed Snatchers

Dale Fife

Illustrated by Sandy Kossin

Houghton Mifflin Company
Boston 1983

Library of Congress Cataloging in Publication Data

Fife, Dale.
 The sesame seed snatchers.

 Summary: Ten-year-old Mike and his best friend
form "The Two Guys Private Eyes" detective agency
and discover how sesame seeds are mysteriously
disappearing from Silas Newton's Wild Red Raspberry
Jelly Factory in San Francisco.
 [1. Mystery and detective stories]   I. Kossin,
Sandy, ill.   II. Title.
 PZ7.F4793Se   1983   [Fic]   83-12630
 ISBN 0-395-34826-9

Printed in the United States of America

v 10 9 8 7 6 5 4 3 2 1

With thanks to
Robin Sands Fife
Allen Sands
Duncan Fife

Contents

The Sesame Seed Snatchers

1
Suky

I'm Mike. Hank is my best friend.

We both live in this old apartment house near Fisherman's Wharf. Hank lives on the first floor, and I live up two flights. In my room, if I stand on my bunk and crane my neck about ninety degrees, I can see Alcatraz out there in the bay, or maybe a freighter sliding under the Golden Gate Bridge bound for Hong Kong, or Singapore, or maybe Manila. All places it's fun to dream about.

It has just turned summer vacation, but Hank and I are not going anywhere. We're trying to find jobs. But who hires kids? Then a week ago I got this Super Spy Kit for my tenth birthday. When I saw the neat disguises, like mustaches and false noses, and the casebook to write in all the facts, and the magnifying glass, I got this idea to start a detective agency, and I talked Hank into joining it.

We call ourselves "The Two Guys Private Eyes," and we advertise by tacking up signs on the bulletin board in Tony Tortolino's Little Supermarket nearby.

Last night we got our first call. Right now Hank and I are waiting to make the connection. I'm passing the time looking through the magnifying glass, examining a patch of weeds that grow through a crack in the sidewalk in front of our apartment.

"Hank," I say, "do you realize how big a load an ordinary ant can carry?"

"Sensational," Hank snorts, shoving his fingers through his rowdy hair. "You're wasting your time spying on ants when we should be hustling a case."

Maybe I should let you in on the fact that

Hank is a pessimist. My dad told me that a pessimist is someone who has to get along with an optimist.

"Do you have to spend your whole life griping?" I ask. "At this very second we're waiting for our first client — Susannah."

The sun struggles through the fog. Hank shrugs out of his red Windbreaker. "Susannah," he snorts. "There can't be anyone living in this century by the name of Susannah. If there is, she's got to be over a hundred years old."

"Is that so?" I shout. "Well, my mother's cousin's middle name is Susannah. She does yoga and stands on her head and she's no hundred years old."

I don't want to admit that I'm wondering about Susannah myself. Her voice on the telephone last night sounded whispery and scared. She would not tell me what the case was about, or where she was calling from. "I read your ad on Tony Tortolino's Little Supermarket bulletin board," was all she said.

Hank's ears are big and flappy. When he gets a new idea they wiggle. They're wiggling now. "I think we should change our line of business. Susannah, whoever she is, isn't coming. She's half an hour late now."

"Give up being detectives?" I say. "It takes time to become famous private eyes. We've just started."

Hank chucks a couple of sourballs into his mouth. He has one in each cheek, and he looks like a case of mumps. "At the rate we're going, summer vacation will be over, and what will we have to brag about to Windy Wendell and the other kids when they come home from Disneyland and Sea World and places like that?"

I think that Hank could be right. "Maybe we could walk dogs," I say.

"Around here?" Hank says. "Everyone walks his own dog."

"I know what," I say. "We can put a note on

4

Tortolino's bulletin board advertising that we'll water plants for people going on vacation."

Hank sneezes. "Anything green gives me hives, and I get itchy. I'm what you call allergic."

"Are you allergic to birds?" I ask.

"I'm not allergic to anything that flies," he says, looking up at the sky.

"There's a sign in Wing Lo's Pet Shop window. He needs someone to clean out birdcages," I say.

Hank unscrambles himself and stands up. "Well, if all we can do is keep house for canaries . . ."

I pocket my magnifying glass and vault to my feet at the very moment that a girl on a skateboard scrunches to a stop, barely missing my toes. She's skinny as a hockey stick, and has a face full of freckles and hair almost as red as a STOP sign.

"The Two Guys Private Eyes?" she asks,

panting. Then, without waiting for an answer, she plunges on, "I'm Susannah. Sorry I'm late. One of the Jellies got stuck in the dumbwaiter and I had to help fish her out."

Jellies? Dumbwaiter?

This is weird, but I'm curious. Hank's eyebrows are meeting. That means he's feeling negative. "We just closed out our detective business. We're into bird maintenance," he growls.

This is when I notice that Susannah's eyes are green. They're flashing. "That's no way to run a business," she shouts. "I've been counting on you to solve the robbery where I live."

"Sorry . . ." Hank begins.

I interrupt. "Where do you live?"

She glances all around. "Silas Newton's Wild Red Raspberry Jelly Factory," she whispers.

I jerk my Super Spy casebook out of my shirt pocket. "Why didn't you say so in the first place?"

Silas Newton's Wild Red Raspberry Jelly Factory is an old brick building, boarded up, just three blocks away. It's close to the wharf near the coffee-bean roasting company and around the corner from the wax museum. It's spooky. Hank and I sometimes go out of our way just to go past it and make up wild stories about it, and here's our chance to get inside.

But Hank's eyebrows are still meeting. "Why is it no one's ever heard of anyone living there besides Mama Fig, unless you count the ghosts that kids say they see. Are you one of the ghosts?" he jokes.

Susannah puts her hands on her hips and yells, "I'm not a ghost, and I do live in the jelly factory, but I'm not supposed to talk about it."

"But it looks like it's all boarded up," Hank says. "How do you get in?"

She looks all around, as if she expects someone is listening, then she whispers, "There's a secret entrance."

At the word *secret* Hank catches fire.

8

"Where?" he asks.

"You'll find out if you take the case," Susannah says.

I wet my pencil on the tip of my tongue. "How can we take the case unless you give us the facts? What's missing?"

She opens her fist. I see a little pile of straw-colored seeds.

"What are they?" Hank asks.

"Sesame seeds," she says. "Not ordinary sesame seeds. They disappear. Vanish."

"If you want them to reappear," Hank says, "get a magician."

Susannah turns on Hank. She throws the seeds at him. "What's it to you if Gus Grabmore gets the old jelly factory away from Mama Fig and turns it into a warehouse to store all the sesame seeds he's scouring the country for to buy right now?"

"Are you talking about *the* Gus Grabmore who calls himself the 'Sesame King?' I ask.

"Right. It's his seeds that are missing."

Hank plucks a sesame seed off his T-shirt. "What are Grabmore's seeds doing in Fig's jelly factory?" he asks.

"It was my dad's idea; he works for Gus Grabmore. He knew that Grabmore had just bought another big batch of seeds and had no place to store them. Fig was broke, so he told her he thought it would be a good idea to rent the empty vat to Grabmore. Now my dad can't sleep for worrying that Fig will lose the jelly factory."

"How?" I ask.

"Grabmore wants to get his hands on the whole building and turn it into a sesame seed warehouse."

"How can he get it? She owns it."

"She's hanging on to it by a shoestring."

"How's that?" I ask.

"The City notified Fig some time ago that the old building had to be brought up to code. She didn't do it."

"Well, why didn't she?" Hank blurts.

"It takes money for that," Susannah flares.

"I still can't see what all the fuss is about," Hank says.

"Well, then, I'll tell you. When Grabmore gets back and finds his seeds are missing, first thing he'll do is call in the police. The City will discover that even though the place is boarded up, Fig never left it, and that she has a few paying guests besides. We'll all be evicted, with no place to go. My dad will be out of work again, and what will the Jellies do?"

"What are Jellies?" I ask.

Susannah clams up.

Nothing gets to Hank like a secret. "How can we get into the place?" he asks. "There's that Mad Watchman who marches around with a baseball bat over his shoulder, just daring anyone to come close."

"Easy," Susannah says. "I'll tell him you're interested in taking music lessons from my dad."

"You said your dad worked for Gus Grabmore," Hank says.

"He does. All night long he makes sesame doughnuts, chocolate marshmallow cookies, and peanut butter cake. Mornings he's himself again, a professor of music."

The case is beginning to sound stranger and stranger. "Why is a professor of music working in a bakery?" I ask.

Susannah sighs. "It was the only job he could get."

"What about his doing his own thing — music?" I ask.

Susannah shakes her head. "No one hires him. To my dad, 'rock' is a stone, and a 'disco' is a place to crack your eardrums. When he was a boy, and the protégé of Silas and Fig Newton, people coaxed him to play melodies on his fiddle. Mama Fig still coaxes. She invited us to stay in the jelly factory until times get better for us. Well, how about it? Are you going to take the case?"

"We charge for our services," Hank says.

"I don't have any money, but my dad brings samples home from the bakery," Susannah says. "This morning he brought strawberry tarts."

Hank's ears are wiggling.

I get the message.

"We'll figure out our strategy and begin tomorrow morning," I say.

Susannah's face lights up. She slides out of her sweater and ties it around her waist as she readies to go home. I read what it says on her yellow T-shirt: CALL ME SUKY.

"Is your name Susannah or Suky?" I ask.

"Both," she says.

"How come?" I ask.

"Some of the Jellies can't say 'Susannah' very well."

"Anyone can say 'Susannah,'" Hank says.

"Not if you don't have teeth," she says, whisking away.

Hank almost chokes on a sourball. "What

has this Suky gotten us into?" he asks.

"The Case of the Disappearing Sesame Seeds," I say, writing it into my casebook.

2
The Invisible Gate

We are in our office early the next morning. It is in the basement laundry, where we keep our Super Spy equipment — an old cigar box full of stubby pencils, the Super Spy rule book, and our disguises — on a shelf next to the detergents and Clorox.

Of necessity our office hours are early. No one is washing and drying at seven A.M.

We're not wearing disguises on this case, but I am carrying my dad's beat-up violin case. Hank is making off-key noises on his piccolo.

"I don't believe we're doing this," he says. "I think this Suky character is putting us on, talking about a secret entrance, something called 'Jellies,' and vanishing sesame seeds."

"I looked up *sesame seed* in the dictionary last night," I say.

"Did it say anything about them disappearing?"

"All it said was that the oil is used for food and to make soap."

"That gives us zero to go on," Hank says.

"Right, but I telephoned my grandmother to ask if she could tell me anything."

"Your grandmother!" Hank snorts. "What would *she* know about it?"

Hank is that way about old people, especially grandparents. He never met his. They're somewhere in the old country.

"Well, my grandmother told me that Newton's Wild Red Raspberry Jelly used to be world famous. People came from all over to buy it. She said that everyone in old San Francisco ate scones with Newton's Wild Red Raspberry Jelly for Sunday breakfast. It was a tradition, like having turkey for Thanksgiving."

Anything older than last week's comic book doesn't interest Hank. His name is really "Heinrich," but don't call him that. He won't answer. He's already halfway out the door.

The fog is as thick as mashed potatoes this morning. It almost blocks out the cable car waiting at the end of the line.

When we reach the jelly factory, we can hardly make out the faded gold lettering across the front that reads

SILAS NEWTON'S WILD RED RASPBERRY

JELLY FACTORY

Hank scrunches deep into his sweater. "What a spooky old building," he says. "If it were mine I'd bulldoze it down."

"It looks kind of sad to me," I say. "I feel sorry for it."

"How can you feel sorry for a worn-out old building?" Hank asks. "It reminds me of the haunted-house movie we saw last week, where the plaster kept falling off the ceiling and hitting people on the head, and the floors gave way, and the walls kept caving in."

"Quiet," I whisper. "I hear footsteps."

"If it's that Mad Watchman, I'm leaving," Hank says, ready to take off.

"It's Suky," I say. "Hi!" I call.

She puts a finger against her mouth to shut me up and beckons us on. I follow, with Hank right behind me.

She leads us down a narrow path alongside the building. It twists through a tunnel of green hedge.

Hank sneezes.

A thorn reaches out and grabs my jeans. I stop to pry myself loose. When I look up, Suky is nowhere.

"She's vanished," I say.

"Let's move out of here," Hank says, sneezing again.

I hear Suky's giggle from the other side of the hedge. "Find the secret gate," she says.

Hank spots it first. Painted green, hidden by overhead vines, we had gone right past it in the fog. Once through it, we are at the bottom of stone steps that lead up to wide double doors. Standing there is the Mad Watchman, wielding a baseball bat.

"STOP! SPIES!" he shouts.

We freeze.

But Suky goes right up to him as if he were as harmless as a pussycat. "They're here to see my dad about music," she says.

Mad Watchman lowers the baseball bat and bows us into the jelly factory.

Once we're inside, I get a strange feeling. It's not today. It's a long time ago, the time my grandmother talks about.

We are in a great shining hall. The carved ceiling is so high it makes me feel that I have shrunk 'way down to the inlaid star in the stone floor. There are marble pillars and gold chairs. Chandeliers of colored glass hang over our heads. Suky presses a switch, and the lights make blue, green, and red patterns on the wood of the walls.

"Am I in a palace?" I ask.

"Not really," Suky says, "but in the old days even the Prince of Lichtenstein came here to buy Silas Newton's Wild Red Raspberry Jelly. And now I'll show you the office of the great Silas Newton."

We stop at a door marked PRESIDENT in foot-high gold letters. As Suky turns the knob and opens the door, I get a flashing glimpse of someone, or something, white and shrunken, busily polishing a roll-top desk. I blink my eyes. It's gone. Did I imagine it? What is this old jelly factory doing to me?

Even Hank is interested as we look at the brass spittoon, the hat tree, and a picture of San Francisco with no high buildings, no TV antennas, but lots of big ships, with sails, in the bay.

Suky points to the picture of a man with a long beard and merry blue eyes. "That's Silas

Newton," she says, "and that's Mama Fig in the picture next to him."

"Why do you call her Mama Fig?" Hank asks.

"In the old days it was San Francisco's nickname for her," Suky says.

Fig has a round face and eyes that smile right into mine.

I run my fingers over the roll-top desk. Something oily sticks to them. I smell it. Furniture polish!

A chill crawls up my back.

Did I or didn't I see a white something polishing the desk?

Suky is watching me.

"Suky, did I see . . ."

She herds us out of the room. "I want to show you the sesame seeds."

3
Ghosts?

We cross a toy bridge to another part of the building and a door marked MAIN BOILING ROOM.

Suky fishes a key from her sweater pocket and fits it into the lock. She hesitates. "I'm not supposed to have this key or even to know where my dad keeps it," she says.

We help shove in the heavy door. It's dark inside.

"There they are," Suky says.

"I can't see a thing," Hank says.

My eyes get used to the pale light coming in through high, half-boarded-up windows. I make out a huge container that reminds me of pictures I've seen of a witch's cauldron, only it's set right into the floor and you can't see its bottom. All around it there are short three-rung ladders. We climb one to look into the vat.

"WOW!" Hank cries. "I didn't know there were this many seeds in all the world!"

Suky climbs up beside me. "Oh no," she wails.

"What's wrong?" I ask.

"More seeds have disappeared," she cries.

I reach down to the seeds. They feel smooth as ivory in my fingers. The half light makes them sort of glow.

"It's my guess rats are getting to them," Hank says.

Suky shakes her head. "Wrong. Rats have been checked out."

I look up at the windows.

"They haven't been open in years," Suky says.

"What's Gus Grabmore's reason for stocking up on so many sesame seeds?" I ask.

"He wants to corner the market. He heard there is going to be a worldwide shortage of them."

Hank and I walk around the vat.

"What does it drain into?" I ask.

"Nothing," Suky says. "Follow me and you'll find out how the vat was used."

She crosses to another part of the room to a huge mechanical contraption. "Let me introduce you to Casey," she says.

"He looks like our man on the moon," Hank says.

Casey is a large shiny metal pot with pipes like a boxer's arms sticking out of his fat sides.

"Casey was very important in the good old days when Newton's Wild Red Raspberry Jelly Factory was about the most important business in the city," Suky says. "People would go out in the country to pick the wild raspberries and sell them to Silas Newton. There was even a 'Wild Raspberry Day,' when whole families took picnic lunches and crossed the bay in ferryboats to pick wild raspberries. The berries all ripened about the same time, so Silas Newton invented Casey the Crusher."

"What could Casey do with a raspberry?" Hank asks.

"He'd be switched on," Suky says. "Berries would be poured into his middle. He'd move his arms up and down, crushing the berries, sending the juice through an overhead pipe that emptied into the vat. See that hole in Casey's head? It's where the overhead pipe used to be."

"I'm way ahead of you," Hank says. "The juice was mixed with sugar in the vat and it all boiled together and made gallons of raspberry jelly."

"Wrong again, Hank," Suky says. "Anyone who knows anything about Newton's Wild Red Raspberry Jelly knows that it was the best jelly in the world, and people stood in lines

three blocks long to get it, because Silas Newton knew that jelly must be cooked in small
batches. Workers with giant dippers ladled it
out of the holding vat into cooking pots, where
it was boiled with sugar in small batches over
in the far corner on that stove that has twenty-
four burners."

"How do you know all this?" I ask.

"Boss told me."

"Who's Boss?"

"The one you call the Mad Watchman."

"How does he know the things you've told
us?"

"He was the head jelly maker."

The whole story is so fantastic that I imagine Casey the Crusher's arms moving up and
down, squeezing the raspberries into juice. I
get a strange feeling that I can smell raspberries at this very moment.

There are so many crocks and tools and bar-
rels in the room that I'm all for exploring, but
Suky says it's time to go. We follow her out.

"Stay right here," she says, locking the door behind us. "Don't move. I've got to take this key back to the hiding place."

"Where's that?" I ask.

She races away without answering.

Hank is sniffing around like a puppy dog. "Funny, but I think I smell raspberries," he says.

"So do I," I say.

"There's something strange going on here," Hank says.

"Rule Number One in my Super Spy book says, '*Investigate.*' Since we both smell raspberries and this factory has been closed for years and years, I say we should follow our noses."

We do. They lead us smack into a door marked AUXILIARY BOILING ROOM.

"What does that mean?" Hank asks.

"The room where we saw the seeds was marked MAIN BOILING ROOM. Maybe this was a boiling room too but not as big," I say, slowly turning the knob and taking a peek.

"What do you see?" Hank asks.

"Nothing but an empty room with a big window, kind of steamed up, that looks into the room where some noise is coming from. Let's go in and try to see what's on the other side of the window."

I stoop 'way over and sneak up, bear fashion, to the window. Hank is right behind me.

We start inching up the wall until we reach the window.

We stiffen.

Whatever they are, whatever we're seeing, it's like Halloween. A bunch of white-haired little old people, with faces that look kind of like wrinkled apples, are busy as elves in a toy shop. All of them have on long white aprons. Some of them are bent 'way over, some have canes, and one is in a wheelchair.

Two of them are pouring what looks and smells like raspberry jelly into jars.

Two of them are putting lids on jars.

Two of them put the jars into an overhead basket. It whizzes across the room on wires to where two more of them are waiting by a cubbyhole, which has a sign that says DUMB-WAITER.

They load the jars into the cubbyhole. They pull a rope. The cubbyhole disappears.

Have Hank and I cracked the time machine? Are we back in the early days of this jelly factory?

Now we hear music.

Hank's eyes bug out. He points to a far corner where there is a piano. "Look," he says. "It's playing. The keys are moving, but no one's sitting there. I told you there were ghosts in this place. I'm crashing out."

He does.

I follow.

We don't stop until we get to where Suky left us.

4
The Mysterious Triangle

Hank shivers. "Let's clear out before Suky gets back," he says. "This place is haunted."

I'm kind of shaken myself, even though I don't believe in ghosts, but I'm not ready to quit. Still I don't want to go on without Hank. I get an idea. "Maybe what we saw are the extraterrestrials you're always talking about."

"E.T.'s here?" Hank says.

"Well, remember the time you were sure you saw a UFO dangling right over the Golden Gate Bridge, and I couldn't talk you out of it?"

"What's that got to do with what we just saw?" Hank asks. "Extraterrestrials wouldn't be floating around making raspberry jelly. They'd have more important things to do."

"I don't understand why Suky hasn't told us about what's going on in the Auxiliary Boiling Room," I say. "The Super Spy book says we must be given all the facts."

"Maybe she doesn't know about what we saw," Hank says. "That's why I lean toward the ghost theory. Ghosts don't appear to just anyone. Suky's probably never seen them . . . wait a minute, Mike. She did talk about something called 'Jellies' and about one of them getting stuck in the dumbwaiter."

"Good thinking, Hank," I say. "We didn't know what a 'dumbwaiter' was then, but now we do."

Hank is so revved up his ears are wiggling again. "Remember why Suky said she was called 'Suky'? She said some of the Jellies couldn't say 'Susannah' because they didn't have teeth. Did you notice if what we saw had teeth?" he asks.

"No, did you?"

"I was too scared to notice," Hank says.

And now Suky comes rushing up to us, all apologies for keeping us waiting.

"Suky," I say, "if we are to go on with this case, we must know who lives here, and where."

"Oh, you're going to meet everyone right away," she says. "They're all in the kitchen fixing their breakfasts. We'll go right past their rooms on the way to the kitchen. Come along."

We follow her through a door marked SUPPLIES FOR RED RASPBERRY JELLY. Suky leads us along a hallway lined with several doors. The first one we stop at has a red and white sign that reads EMPTY JARS.

"This is Hungry Jack's room," Suky says.

"Why do you call him Hungry Jack, and why is he living in a room that says 'Empty Jars'?" asks Hank.

"He's an orphan. One day he helped Mama

Fig home with groceries from Tony Tortolino's Little Supermarket, where he works. He told her he had no family anywhere. She invited him to stay for dinner, and he never left. We call him 'Hungry Jack' because he's always hungry."

I peek through the half-open door. The room is as messy as my mom says mine is. The walls are plastered with posters of food — spaghetti, chocolate sundaes, French fries . . .

"This next room is Ms. Trill's," Suky says, moving on to a door marked SUGAR. Through a crack I get a glimpse of gypsy colors and sandals.

"She's an opera singer," Suky says, thrusting out her arms in a dramatic pose.

"Why is an opera star living in the sugar storeroom of a jelly factory?" Hank asks.

"Because Hungry Jack told Mama Fig about the notice Ms. Trill tacked on Tony Tortolino's Supermarket bulletin board. It said, 'I'm a lonely stranger in a big city. I need a friend.' Mama Fig invited Ms. Trill to dinner. She didn't leave either."

"Sounds like your Mama Fig takes in strays like some people take in cats," Hank says.

Suky hurries ahead to the next room. The door is shut. A sign that hangs from the knob says KEEP OUT! A sign over the door reads PARAFFIN.

"What's that mean?" Hank asks.

"All Newton's Wild Red Raspberry Jelly glasses were sealed with paraffin," Suky says. "This is Harry Handsom's room. He's the latest guest, a friend of Ms. Trill's, an actor between engagements. That's all I know about him. And now here's the kitchen."

The door is marked TESTING ROOM. Underneath the sign, written in purple ink, is the instruction *"speak softly — flowers asleep."*

Hank looks at it and rolls his eyes at me.

"I'll tell Mama Fig you're here," Suky says. "Be back in a minute."

Hank plops another sourball into his mouth. "Nothing that we've seen adds up to anything," he says.

"It does to me," I say.

"What?"

"The Mysterious Triangle," I say.

"What's that?"

"Well, as I see it, the three guests we've heard about, Hungry Jack, Ms. Trill, and Harry Handsom, are all tied together."

"How do you figure that?"

"Notice that Hungry Jack *offered* to help Mama Fig home with her groceries from the Supermarket. He stayed on. *Next*, Ms. Trill puts a notice on the bulletin board of the same Super. Hungry Jack tells Mama Fig about it, and Ms. Trill comes here. Then Ms. Trill tells Harry Handsom. Now *he's* here."

"I get it," Hank says. "The Mysterious Triangle infiltrates the jelly factory. But why?"

"If my theory is on target, they could be

stooges hired by Gus Grabmore to steal the seeds. When enough seeds are missing, Grabmore will call in the police and blame the theft on Fig. She'll be in double trouble because the police will now discover she has 'paying guests' in a building that is boarded up and supposed to be empty because it hasn't been brought up to code."

"I get it," Hank says. "Fig is now in a tight spot. Grabmore offers her a mini price for the building. She's forced to give up Newton's Wild Red Raspberry Jelly Factory."

"Right on," I say. "And Grabmore will have a gigantic storehouse for his tons of sesame seeds."

Hank punches the air with his fist. "So let's get on with the job and do something," he says, just as Suky opens the door to the kitchen.

5
Suspects

The kitchen is a cozy clutter of baskets and plants and everyone doing his own thing.

Suky introduces us all around.

Hungry Jack turns out to be a bony kid with thick glasses, hair that sticks out like a porcupine's quills, and shoes big as tennis racquets. He's busy opening an unlabeled can. "Anyone want sauerkraut for breakfast?" he shouts. "I thought I was opening peaches."

"He gets to bring bent and unlabeled cans home from Tony Tortolino's Supermarket," Suky explains as she trots us over to where Ms. Trill is pouring yogurt over a dish of granola. Her orange-colored hair floats around her face like a shampoo ad in a TV commercial.

"Be my guest," she says in a voice that kind of sings, as she holds the granola box out to us. We back away.

Harry Handsom looks like his name. He's eating a chocolate bar and cheese for breakfast. He doesn't offer us any.

Mama Fig's smile, which is like the sun coming out of the fog, is all I see at first. She's round and bouncy in a purple-flowered muumuu. Her silvery hair is wound round and round like a beehive on top of her head. "I've been looking for a couple of strong boys like you," she sort of bellows. "Come with me."

We follow her to a row of plants on a shelf beneath a window. "Good morning, Fern," she says. "You're drooping again."

I look around to see who Fern is. Then I see she's talking to a sad-looking plant.

"Fern's a bit on the heavy side," she tells us.

"Will you boys help move her to intensive care?"

Ms. Trill comes tripping over to us. "Fern isn't sick," she says. "She just doesn't like sitting next to that pushy cactus. Move her next to the little pink geranium. She likes the geranium."

We do as Ms. Trill says. I think she bosses nice Mama Fig around.

The door swings open and in comes Professor Freebee. I recognize him right away by his baker's white suit and starched white hat. Suky introduces her dad to us, telling him we are interested in music. His eyes light up and he shakes my hand so hard my fingers ache. He gives Suky a big bag that turns out to be filled with chocolate brownies . . . Hank and I take three apiece.

Suky rushes to take her dad a cup of coffee, and he sits in a rocking chair and begins to read the morning newspaper. Right away he

41

lets out a groan. "Listen to what Terry Trifle says in his gossip column:

'Gus Grabmore, the would-be sesame seed king, who has been hopping from state to state, buying sesame seeds, is due back, in his private plane, on Saturday.'"

For a moment everyone freezes. Then Mama Fig drops into a chair. Her eyes look big and scared. "He said he wouldn't be back until after the Fourth of July. He must have heard about our secret."

She looks around the room. "I can't believe anyone here would have given it away."

Harry Handsom jumps to his feet. He comes to Mama Fig, arms opened wide. "Dear Mama Fig, be assured that not one of us could be guilty of such a heinous crime."

I nudge Hank. "Some ham actor."

Hungry Jack leaps across the room and sits on the arm of Mama Fig's chair. "You know I would give my life for you."

Ms. Trill rakes her orange hair and wails, "My lips have been sealed about the great secret..."

I corner Suky. "What's all this about a big secret?" I ask.

She practically shoves Hank and me out of the room. "Wait for me," she says, and then slams the door shut.

Hank and I stand in the hallway and try to make some sense out of what we have just heard.

"One thing I'm sure of now," I say. "Those three paying guests make up the Mysterious Triangle. Their reactions to the newspaper report were mighty phony."

"Right," Hank says.

"My deduction is that Grabmore is returning early because the Mysterious Triangle got word to him about the secret."

"Agreed," Hank says. "But what *is* the secret and why didn't Suky tell us about it? She hires us to solve the mystery of seeds that disappear, but we're shooed away as soon as there is talk about some great secret."

A light goes on in my brain. "Hank, maybe we were looking right at the secret."

"Where? What?" he asks.

"In the Auxiliary Boiling Room," I say. "Maybe we stumbled on the 'Jellies' Suky hinted at, and maybe they're the secret. Let's go back and find out."

"How can we tell what they are?" Hank asks.

"By looking to see if they have teeth," I say.

"I'm scared to go back," Hank says. "Aren't you?"

"No, just terrified. Are you game?"

"Okay, but if I don't come back, I hope someone tells my mother what became of me."

6
The Secret

We streak down the hall, over the toy bridge, and creep up on the Auxiliary Boiling Room. I hear the piano. It's playing my grandmother's favorite song, "My Wild Irish Rose."

We sneak through the door and shinny up to the window.

We see an impossible sight.

It's like the Haunted House in Disneyland.

The people with the "dried apple faces" are dancing.

They're laughing.

I can see into the mouth of one dancing close to the window.

"Look, Hank, no teeth."

Hank's teeth are chattering. I've got goose-bumps.

"Let's get out of here before they see us," Hank croaks.

I agree.

But before we can move a muscle something grabs hold of us.

I squirm and kick my feet.

No use.

I look up.

It's Mad Watchman.

"SPIES!" he shouts and drags us into the next room.

The music stops.

The dancing stops.

The dried apple faces surround us.

"What are you doing here?" Mad Watch-man shrieks.

I tell the truth. "We're private detectives. Suky hired us to find out where the sesame seeds are disappearing to."

At that, the dried apple faces with cotton

hair grin and come in closer.

Why, they're just old people! Very old people. The oldest people I've ever seen.

Hank finds his voice. "We thought maybe you were ghosts, or from outer space, or maybe we'd cracked the time barrier."

That makes the old people nudge one another and laugh. Even Mad Watchman chuckles. "They're the Jellies," he tells us. "They've come to help Fig."

"What is a Jelly?" I ask.

"This is coffee break time," Mad Watchman says, leading us to a table and starting to explain. "All of these good people once worked right here in Newton's Wild Red Raspberry Jelly Factory. That was when it was the greatest attraction this side of New York City.

"They liked working here, and liked each other so much they formed a club and called themselves 'The Jolly Jellies.' "

The little old man in the wheelchair interrupts. " 'Jumping Jellies' would have been a better name, we had such good times."

A lady with lavender bows in her white hair says, "We kept on meeting even though some of us were in retirement homes, or with our children, places old people go to live whether they want to or not."

She brings us each a scone dripping with wild red raspberry jelly and topped with cream.

One bite and I know why anyone who has tasted Newton's Wild Red Raspberry Jelly can't forget it.

An old man wearing thick eyeglasses and carrying a cane says, "When we found out that our Fig was in trouble, we started to think what we could do to help her. We came up with the idea of bringing back the jelly factory as it was in its heyday. We knew if we were successful, everyone in San Francisco would rally to Fig's cause and help save the building."

He waves his cane at the shelves of jelly

glasses all filled to the brim with wild red raspberry jelly. "We've got enough made to open up on the Fourth of July with a good old-fashioned 'scone and jelly' morning like we had in the old days."

Boss Watchman pounds his fist on the table. "We'll have firecrackers and music like we used to. Professor Freebee was just a boy in those days, but he played his fiddle and we danced many a jig. Once people hear about it, everyone in the city will want to come, and a lot of tourists besides. We'll mow Gus Grabmore down. Won't he be surprised when he gets back?"

Hank looks at me and I know he is thinking the same thing I am. None of these old people know that Gus Grabmore will be back home by Saturday — before the great Fourth of July they are planning.

I can see, too, that for the first time Hank is interested in someone old. "We've got to do something for them," he says as we start to leave. "Just one thing more, though. How do those piano keys go up and down without anyone sitting there?"

"I remember about that now," I say. "My grandmother once told me she had a piano like that. She called it a 'player piano.' "

"Great idea," Hank says. "If we had one, we could be musicians without taking lessons."

I guess he must be thinking about his piccolo.

"Those old folks had some good ideas after all," he says.

7
Suspect Number One

Suky is upset because we found out about the Jellies without her.

"I couldn't tell you," she says. "It was a spectacular secret that could work only if it was kept a secret. But now that it's out and Gus Grabmore is rushing home, all the work the Jellies did polishing this old factory and making jelly will be for nothing."

"Unless we can solve the mystery of the disappearing seeds before he gets here," Hank says.

"We haven't had a chance until now to really go into the case," I say.

Suky, who has looked sad, brightens a little. "How will you begin?" she asks.

"Rule Number Five in my Super Spy book says, '*Consider everyone guilty until proved innocent!*' That means Fig's paying guests. We'll have to trail them," I say.

"Fig won't like that. She trusts everyone."

"She still thinks we're music students. Don't blow our cover," I say. "We'll need your help."

"You can count on me," Suky says. "I'll keep tabs on their comings and goings."

"Mike," Hank says, "it's my opinion we should check the outside of the building before we start trailing anyone."

"Right," I say. "We'll begin at once."

The great Wild Red Raspberry Jelly Factory is on a corner, with a fenced-in, weedy, vacant lot next to it.

"There's always a secret door in a detective story," Hank says.

We inspect the building from one end to the

other. We do not find anything. All we come across are weeds, runty bushes, and old junk. Hank is sneezing from the dust. We have stickers in our hair. Ants are crawling over us. But we find no clues.

We collapse on a tree stump.

"There is no way anyone can get into the place," I say. "That proves it's got to be an inside job."

"If you're sticking to your 'Mysterious Triangle' theory, I think we should begin with Harry Handsom. He looks like a phony to me," Hank says.

"A phony is not necessarily a criminal," I say. "It just makes him a suspect. I say we should start with Hungry Jack."

"That poor orphan? Suky says he doesn't go anyplace but to Tony Tortolino's Little Supermarket where he works."

"Precisely why we should follow him. In detective stories it's always the least likely person who turns out to be the guilty one.

THE SESAME SEED SNATCHERS

Look at the evidence. He brought Fig's groceries home and never left. How do we know
he's an orphan? He could be working for Gus
Grabmore and so put himself in a perfect spot
to make trouble for Fig."

"I'll go along with your deduction," Hank
says. "What disguises shall we wear?"

"None," I say. "Everyone goes into super-
markets. Hungry Jack won't think it's strange
if he spots us."

We decide to drop our musical props off at
home on the way to the Super, so it's almost
noon when we get there. It's Thursday. That
means it's Tony Tortolino's Little Supermarket's Big Sales Day.

"How are we going to find Hungry Jack in
all this mob?" Hank asks.

"Suky says he's in charge of sweeping up.
All we need to do is to walk down one aisle
and up another until we spot him."

We hike from alphabet soup to gingersnaps,

and from health foods to the Xerox machine, but we do not see Jack.

We're back in health foods when we spot a sign that says SUPER SALE ON SESAME SEED PRODUCTS.

We stare at five shelves filled with sesame products.

Hank picks up a package called "Sesame Seed Helper." It seems that it helps hamburgers, meatballs, and even yesterday's hash.

We discover that sesame seeds are dessert for the birds.

I shake a bottle of sesame oil. Hank finds sesame cookies, sesame candies, sesame gum. Yesterday we thought "sesame" was just the name of a street. Today we find this supermarket jammed with sesame products.

"Wow!" Hank says. "Sesame seeds are big business here."

"Hungry Jack could be the market's sesame seed connection," I say.

"There he is now," Hank whispers, pointing to someone sweeping.

But it isn't Hungry Jack.

"He's been promoted to boxes and crates," the sweeper says, flipping a thumb in the direction of the back room.

Promoted!

Our suspicions deepen.

We streak for the back room even though a sign says KEEP OUT.

We hide behind a stack of crates.

We spot Hungry Jack. He is staggering under a box piled so high with spinach that we cannot see his face. We recognize him by his big feet.

We trail him through the supermarket.

We peek from behind a mountain of carrots while he stacks the spinach.

When he heads back to the storeroom, we are right behind him.

We watch as he picks up a large bag.

He shoulders it and heads straight for the health foods.

We follow.

Six customers and their carts come between us.

We make an end run around them.

We bump into one of the carts.

It bumps into the cart ahead, which rear-ends the one ahead of it.

Carts pile up. They fill the aisle. There is a traffic jam in the health food department.

I feel an iron grip on my shoulder. I look up into the angry face of a giant who has a badge marked SUPERVISOR pinned onto his shirt. "This market is not a playpen," he says, propelling us to the door.

"Well, we flubbed that one," Hank says. "Just when we were on to something really big."

I remind Hank of Rule Number Six in my

Super Spy book: "*If at first you don't succeed, try, try again.*"

We hide behind a meat truck parked alongside one of the big market windows. The Supervisor has disappeared. We don't want to tangle with him again, but we don't want to miss the chance to see what Hungry Jack is doing in the health food department with the suspicious-looking bag.

We sneak back into the store under cover of a side of beef being carried to the butcher's block.

We rush for the health food section and creep up behind Hungry Jack.

He swivels.

When he sees us, he jumps back and drops the sack. It breaks.

The Supervisor comes on the run.

"Pretend we're customers," I whisper to Hank as I grab a sesame candy bar.

Hank pulls a box of sesame sticks from the shelf.

The Supervisor glares at us and follows us to the checkstand. He stands there, hands on hips, as the clerk rings up $1.98 on the cash register.

Hank reaches into his pockets. He pulls them inside out. Empty.

I feel into mine. I find a dime.

"Aha!" the Supervisor says. "Shoplifters."

I'm shaking in my Nikes.

Hank is grinding his teeth.

Then I see Hungry Jack beside us. "They're my friends," he says, handing the cashier the $1.98.

We slink out of the store.

We are at the bottom of the heap.

I take out my casebook and begin to cross Hungry Jack's name off the suspect list. "He's clean," I say. "He saved us."

"Maybe he saved himself," Hank says. "We didn't have to pay for the things we had. We hadn't taken them outside the store."

"I don't follow you," I say.

"The way I see it," Hank says, "he suspected we were trailing him. He probably thought we had something on him and didn't want us questioned."

"Exactly what have we got on Hungry Jack?" I ask.

"Maybe nothing, but I go with the theory he tried to put us off the trail by being a good guy. That sack might have held sesame seeds stolen from the jelly factory that Hungry Jack sold to the supermarket. I wish we knew for sure."

"I do."

"How?"

"The sack split wide open when Hungry Jack dropped it."

"What was in it?"

"Beans."

8
Suspect Number Two

Hank and I need to get information about our next suspect. We find Suky in the kitchen with Mama Fig, who is making posters to advertise the Fourth of July hoopla at the jelly factory. Suky is helping her. The kitchen walls are covered with posters of raspberries — everything from a raspberry plant dripping with huge red berries to a poster of a gigantic scone, doused in raspberries. It's enough to make us hungry.

"I'm going to put them in every store on the wharf and hang them all over town," Suky says.

Mama Fig offers us red apples. "If you're here for your music lessons, Professor Freebee is still asleep," she says. "The poor man works so hard all night long braiding dough and frosting cakes, he's still snoring. I can hear him through these walls. Suky, you better wake him up and tell him his new pupils are here."

Hank and I back away.

"Will do," Suky says, and the three of us escape to the hall.

"We came to ask you about Ms. Trill and her singing habits," I say.

"Opera stars have strange singing hours," Suky says. "They wear odd costumes. At least Ms. Trill does."

"What's her first name?" I ask, pencil poised over my casebook.

"Tillie," Suky says.

"Well then, when Tillie Trill leaves to warble in an opera does she tote something, like maybe a sack or a box?" I ask.

"She always has a big bag hanging from her shoulder," Suky says.

"How does she travel?" I ask. "By car? Bicycle?"

"Different ways," Suky says. "She walks over to the Pizza Shack on the next corner and catches a bus, or maybe a cable car, depending on where she's singing."

"We can't hang around the Pizza Shack all day," Hank says. "Our time is valuable."

"I happen to know that she's singing today around four o'clock. It's almost that now. You might be lucky enough to see her."

Before we take off, Suky gives each of us a chocolate chip cookie big as a dinner plate. "My dad brought them home this morning. I saved them for you," she says.

We hike to the pizza corner, eating our giant cookies. We wait and we wait. The cookies have whetted our appetites and the good pizza smells sneak out of the Pizza Shack and attack us. It's almost more than we can stand.

"Suky must be wrong about Tillie Trill," I say. "It doesn't look as if she's singing tonight.

We might as well go home and grab something to eat."

And then we see her. But we don't recognize her until she jumps into a taxi. We don't recognize her because she does not look like Tillie Trill. She is wearing a red cutaway coat over black pants. On her head she has a black top hat and she has a mechanical monkey tied around her neck.

The taxi whizzes away and we start to jog toward home.

"What opera is Tillie Trill singing, do you think, dressed like that?" I ask Hank.

"I've never been to the opera," Hank says.

"My grandmother goes to the opera," I say. "I'll ask her."

When I get home I telephone my grandmother. She tells me she never heard of an opera in which a singer carries a mechanical monkey around her neck.

I am on my ninth meatball and second helping of mashed potatoes when I get a telephone call from Suky. She sounds excited. "I just answered a call for Tillie Trill. I took the message. Want to hear it?"

"Fire away," I say.

"Here it comes," Suky says. "Tomorrow . . . four P.M. . . . clown . . . Big Timber Montana order . . . contact Sammy . . . delivery ten . . ."

"Read it again," I shout. "I'll write it down."

After I hang up, I eat my chocolate pie while running down to Hank's apartment.

"*Wow!*" he yells when he hears the news. "Contact at last."

The next day we are at the Pizza Shack half an hour early. We watch the action on the street. I spy a clown on the other side coming from the direction of the jelly factory. I nudge Hank. "The telephone message that Suky told us about mentioned 'clown.' "

"The clown's got a canvas bag over the shoulder," Hank says.

"And a monkey around the neck," I say. "It's got to be Tillie Trill."

We scoot out of sight behind a rubbish can.

But Tillie Trill does not cross over to our side of the street. She turns a corner.

Hank and I pop out from our hiding place, race across the street, and turn the corner just in time to see Tillie Trill disappear into a crowded cable car.

We hop onto the outside step and dig out our fares for the conductor. We keep a guarded eye on Ms. Trill, all the while trying to decode the telephone call.

"The message used the word *clown*," Hank says. "I think Tillie Trill was told what to wear so the contact, Sammy, would recognize her."

I take a stronger grip on the post I am clinging to as we fly around a curve. " 'Delivery ten' could mean the quantity of seeds ordered by 'Big Timber Montana,' who sounds like a big-time operator," I say.

"We could be onto a real big scam," Hank says, offering me a sourball and tossing another one into his mouth. "Imagine the look on Windy Wendell's face when he hears about our solving the great sesame seed mystery. Maybe our pictures will be in the newspaper. Terry Trifle will probably write all about us in his column. Who'll listen to Windy Wendell's hotshot stories after that?"

We grin around our juicy sourballs as the cable car dingdongs down a hill.

When it stops at the entrance to Chinatown, Tillie Trill and a crowd of passengers get off. We leap to the pavement and run after her. We almost lose her in the street of gawking tourists. We catch up when she stops before a building that has a restaurant upstairs.

We duck behind a stand of litchi nuts.

A man slides out of the shadows.

He makes contact with Tillie Trill. He reaches into his pocket and takes out his wallet. We see him count out some bills and give them to her. She hands over the canvas sack she's been carrying.

"She's handed him the evidence," Hank says.

The two of them disappear up the stairs.

"We've got to follow them," I say.

We do, legs shaking.

At the top there's a big dining room. No one pays any attention to us. We sit down at a table for two.

"We'll have to order something," I say. "How much money do you have?"

"Three dollars," Hank says.

I reach into my pocket and count my change. "We've got five dollars and thirty cents between us," I say.

We scan the menu. The only food we can order for that is one dish of chop suey, or a plate of pot stickers. We don't know what pot stickers are so we decide on the chop suey.

When the waiter, one eyebrow raised, asks what we want, we tell him that we want one order of Sub Gum Chop Suey and two plates.

We glance all around the big room, but we don't see Tillie Trill. We hear a noisy party in a private dining room. We can't see into it because two screens close it off from the big room.

"She's got to be in there," I tell Hank.

Our chop suey arrives, along with chopsticks and two fortune cookies.

We've never used chopsticks before but we manage to spear the chop suey and deliver it to our mouths.

We pocket the fortune cookies, count out money to pay our bill, and, when no one is looking, slide out of our chairs and slink across the room to peek around the Chinese screens. We see a long table with some grownups, but mostly kids.

There's a loud RA — TA — TA and Tillie Trill leaps into the room from a door on the opposite side. "I'm looking for Sammy," she tweets. "Is Sammy here?"

A kid, red-faced, gets to his feet.

Everyone claps.

Tillie Trill talks to the monkey: "Maxie, clap for Sammy."

Maxie bangs two cymbals together.

"Sammy," Tillie Trill says, "I have a message for you from Bigtimber, Montana. Do you know anyone in Bigtimber?"

Sammy grins, showing a front tooth missing. "My Uncle Watson lives in Bigtimber."

Tillie Trill claps her hands. "Let's all give Uncle Watson a hand."

Everyone does, including Maxie on the cymbals.

"Here's the message," Tillie Trill says, "from Uncle Watson in Bigtimber." She sings:

"Happy Birthday, dear Sammy,
Happy tenth birthday to you."

"It's one of those singing telegrams," Hank says.

A waiter brings in a birthday cake with ten candles. The "contact" man opens the bag Tillie had given him. He passes around whistles, paper hats, and balloons.

Hank and I sneak away amid all the celebrating.

We are disgusted.

Back on the street we find that we do not have enough money left to take either a cable car or a bus.

We start to walk . . . uphill . . . downhill . . . uphill . . . down . . .

By the time we get home our feet feel as if we'd walked over red-hot coals. We flop down on the apartment house steps.

I remember the fortune cookies and pull mine from my pocket. It's all smashed, but I eat it. Then I read my fortune. "Listen to this," I say.

" 'EVERY OYSTER DOES NOT HAVE A PEARL.
KEEP DIGGING.'

"I guess that's telling me to keep on trying,"
I say.

Hank breaks open his fortune cookie. "Do
you realize, Mike, that we have just one more
suspect — Harry Handsom?"

"We need only one," I say, "if it's the right
one. We'll tackle his case first thing in the
morning. By the way, what does your fortune
cookie say?"

Hank reads it and groans. He hands it to me,
and I read:

" 'IF RUNG IN LADDER BREAKS,
DANGEROUS TO TAKE NEXT STEP.' "

9
Defeated

And now it's Friday.

Black Friday. Gus Grabmore is due home tomorrow.

This morning, in our office, even I am pessimistic. So far we have uncovered no clues about where the sesame seeds are disappearing to.

"How are we going to follow an out-of-work actor?" Hank asks. "Even Suky doesn't know much about him."

"She knows this much — Harry Handsom goes to the bank every day."

"Why's an out-of-work actor going to the bank every day?" Hank asks.

"He must have money," I say. "We've got to find out where he gets it."

"Suky said that he never leaves the jelly factory until the sun comes out. This time of year mornings are foggy, so it may be noon before he gets going."

"That might be a clue as to what he's up to," I say. "Just why does he wait until the sun comes out before he goes over to the bank?"

"Maybe he's allergic to fog," Hank says.

"Suky said he travels from place to place. She says that's the life of an actor."

"It's also the life of a bum," Hank says. "Maybe he rides the rails. I think he's a dangerous character. Did you ever notice his eyes? They're sharp enough to cut glass. Remember the picture we were looking at in the post office of the Brink's robber they never caught? He's got the same slick hair. We'd better wear disguises. If he recognizes us, he might put his mob on our trail."

"Since he's an actor," I say, "it will be hard

to find a disguise that will fool him. I think we should go as mimes. There are so many of them around the wharf he won't notice us."

My Super Spy Kit has pots of make-up. By the time we're finished with it, our faces are dead white, our mouths are red as catsup, and we have smudges of black hiding our eyebrows.

There is a knock on the door.

It's Suky.

When she gets over laughing at our make-up, she hands us some Danish that her dad brought home from the bakery this morning.

"I thought I'd let you know that Harry Handsom just left for the wharf. Early for him."

"The sun must be out," I say.

"It is," she says.

Now she looks worried. "Another thing. My dad measured the seeds in the vat. They're down another inch."

Bad news!

"We'll be on our way," I say, and we rush out, eating the Danish on the way to the wharf. It isn't easy to eat with all the goo on our faces, but we manage.

We spot Harry Handsom immediately. He's leaning against the door of the bank, and he's carrying a canvas sack.

"That sack isn't big enough to carry many seeds," Hank says.

"It's the kind I've seen the gas station man and the candy shop manager take to the bank," I say.

Just then it's time for the bank to open, and Harry Handsom is the first one inside.

A dozen or more people follow.

By the time Hank and I decide whether to risk Harry Handsom's recognizing us, if we go into the bank, he comes out. He strolls around the wharf. We follow ten steps behind.

He stops to talk to a fisherman mending a net. We duck behind a crab pot to watch.

"He could be making a connection," Hank says.

We move in closer. We hide behind a sign that says FRESH BAIT.

We're close enough so we can hear what Harry Handsom and the fisherman are saying.

"I hear Pier Thirty-nine is jumping. Maybe you can unload more there," the fisherman says.

"I'll stick it out here," Harry Handsom says. "Who knows who'll show up, and it's near the bank."

Hank grabs my arm. "Did you hear that? We're onto something big."

A tour bus pulls up across the square. The doors open, and people spill out. They're wearing ten-gallon hats and boots.

"Texas tourists," the fisherman says. "Take 'em on."

Harry ambles over to the bus.

We follow. We infiltrate the crowd so Harry doesn't see us.

But the kids do.

We'd forgotten about our make-up until a crowd of them surrounds us.

"Hey, you mimes, do something."

That is something that had not occurred to us. We panic.

A voice saves us. "Look! A balloon man," a kid yells.

Everybody looks, including Hank and me.

It's Harry Handsom. He's blowing up a huge green balloon.

"It must be a signal of some kind," Hank says.

Harry Handsom begins to twist the balloon. First one end, then the other. He holds it up. It's a dachshund. He throws it into the air. Kids scramble for it.

Then he pulls a cap from his pocket and puts it on his head. It reads HANDSOM'S ANIMALS.

"I've got a quarter. Will you make a cat?" a boy asks.

He makes a purple cat.

A kid tugs at his dad. "I want a panda," he cries.

Handsom makes a panda.

The kid's dad gives Handsom a dollar.

A man hands him ten dollars. "How about five Miss Piggies?" he asks.

Handsom fishes in his pocket for five pink balloons. Presto, five Miss Piggies.

He makes a lion, a giraffe, an elephant, and six rabbits.

"How about an alligator?" asks a woman with a little girl in tow. "We're from Florida."

"Okay," Handsom says. "I've got just enough breath left for one alligator."

The crowd fades away.

All but a ragged little kid. He holds up a penny. "Could I have a dog?" he asks. "You don't need to make a big one. A little one is good enough."

Harry Handsom makes that kid the biggest brown hound you can imagine. He takes the penny. "Thanks for your business," he says to the kid.

Harry Handsom's pockets are bulging with money. He turns and walks straight to the bank.

Hank and I sort of slink away.

We go to a nearby gas station and wash our faces.

"He knew who we were," I say.

"Only a real actor would keep from letting on," Hank says.

"My Super Spy rule book says that to be detectives you have to understand people. We've goofed on all three suspects. You know what that proves?"

"What?"

"We'd better take a job cleaning out birdcages."

"We'll have to tell Suky," Hank says.

"I'd rather be shot," I say. "Do you realize that Gus Grabmore arrives here tomorrow?"

"We shouldn't have taken the case in the

first place," Hank says. "We should have told Suky to hire real detectives. We were too anxious to show off to Windy Wendell and the kids at school."

"I hate to tell you this," I say. "Windy Wendell sent postcards to some of the kids. He wrote them while he was flying in a balloon over the smoking volcano at Mt. St. Helens."

Our steps are slower than molasses in January as we near Newton's Wild Red Raspberry Jelly Factory.

10
Stakeout

"What kind of detectives are you?" Suky shouts at us. "You want to give up on the case just before the deadline!"

Hank shuffles his feet. "Nothing we've tried to do has worked out," he says.

"We feel stupid," I say.

"That's a good sign," Suky says. "In detective stories the detective always looks stupid just before he solves the crime."

"Our case is different," I say. "We've looked stupid right along."

"I had a stupid dream last night," Hank says. "It was more like a nightmare. There was a monster in the jelly factory and it was gobbling the sesame seeds."

"Monster!" I explode. "Don't tell me you believe in them, too."

"Well, not really, but it seemed real. It had six legs and its color was brown."

"Count me out if you're planning on trapping it," I say.

Suky isn't laughing. "This is an old building. Sometimes I hear strange noises."

"It could be something inhuman," Hank says.

"My grandmother's house is old," I say. "When I hear noises my grandmother says that its old bones are creaking."

Hank hangs on to the monster theory. "A monster would have to come and go. There could be some kind of entrance we've missed."

"One thing we haven't tried is a stakeout," I admit.

"We haven't anything to lose," Hank says.

Suky is enthusiastic. "Let's stage it early in the morning when everyone in the jelly factory is asleep, and just before the Jellies come to work."

"How can we disguise ourselves from a monster?" Hank asks.

"Got it," I say. "I saw a show on TV that told how the army uses shrubs and flowers as camouflage."

Hank balks. "You mean we're supposed to disguise ourselves as rosebushes and lilies? I'm allergic. I'll sneeze and give us away."

"Well, you can go as a garbage can," Suky says.

"Okay, let's perfect our strategy and give it our all," I say.

At five in the morning, the lot is as quiet as a graveyard. There is no wind, no fog.

I have oak leaves sprouting from my T-shirt and jeans.

Suky has ivy wound around and around her.

Hank is in a trash can that Suky smuggled out of the jelly factory.

I brief them: "Hank, you watch the roof of the jelly factory. Your monster might escape through the smokestack."

I tell Suky to keep her eyes on the high weeds and bushes. "Report the slightest movement," I say. "I'll keep an ear to the ground. I've read that you can hear footsteps, even light ones, from far away."

We settle in.

Even though I don't believe in monsters, my heart thumps. What if there is some unidentified creature in the old building that can exist on seeds?

We wait.

Nothing happens.

We are still waiting at six o'clock when a church bell rings nearby.

I can see that Suky's ivy is beginning to sag.

I get out my magnifying glass and look for footprints.

All I see is ants.

I watch one carrying a load twice its size. I wonder where it is going. Where it came from.

A long line of ants is marching right under my magnifying glass. They march like soldiers toward the jelly factory.

I see a second line of ants. They are marching away from the jelly factory. They are carrying something in their jaws. The something is as big as they are — or even bigger.

I signal Hank to join me.

He tries to get out of the trash can. It falls over, with him in it, and rolls across the ground, making a racket.

Suky shouts, "QUIET!" and yanks him out of the can.

I follow the ants heading toward the jelly factory. They aren't carrying anything. They lead me to the foundation of the factory.

"What's up?" asks Hank, coming up beside me.

"Help me pull the weeds away from the bricks so we can see what these ants are doing," I say.

The weeds have stickers and burrs. With Suky's help we finally clear them away from the foundation. And there, right before our startled eyes, we see a small pile of sesame seeds.

"Would you look at those ants!" Hank says as we watch them scamper, like mountain climbers, over the hill of seeds.

"Where did those seeds come from?" Suky asks.

I'm scanning the foundation when I spy a tiny crack. A seed is just sifting out of it.

"Look!" I yell.

Hank gets out his penknife. He chips madly away at the mortar until we loosen a brick.

I peer inside. It's too dark to see anything. Suky hands me her flashlight.

"I don't know for sure," I say, "but I think what I'm seeing is the very bottom of the vat."

"It sure is," Hank says, taking a look. "All we could see up in the boiling room was the top of it. Wow, it's leaking seeds into the basement!"

Suky lets out a scream. "That means that the missing seeds are in there."

She takes off like a rocket. "I'm going to tell Fig that the Two Guys Private Eyes solved the case."

Soon everyone — Fig, Boss Watchman, Harry Handsom, Ms. Trill, Hungry Jack, Suky, and her dad — rushes down. Some of them are in their bathrobes. Everyone takes a peek through the hole in the foundation. They shout for joy.

Boss Watchman nods his head. "The vat is ancient. It rusted. The weight of the seeds caused it to give way."

Suky's dad grins ear to ear. "The only seeds missing are the few that trickled to the outside.

The ants will have a good winter on them."

I flash the light through the opening and beam it all around the basement. "It's deep in sesame seeds," I say.

Suky's dad nods. "Gus Grabmore may have a little trouble gathering up his seeds, but there they are."

Suky looks happy. "We won't ever have to move. We can all stay in this wonderful factory forever."

"Cause to celebrate," Fig says.

Boss Watchman helps Hank and me replace the brick we had taken out of the foundation. We shore up the crack so no more seeds can escape.

When we reach the kitchen, it is jumping.

The Jellies have now heard the news. Some of them are doing a square dance to the tune of Professor Freebee's fiddle. He's taken off his baker's suit and put on a blue jacket with brass buttons. Now he looks like a real professor of music.

Harry Handsom is calling the dance:
"Swing your lady to the right,
Swing to the left . . ."

The little lady with the lavender bows in her hair grabs Hank for a partner and Fig grabs me.

Round and round we go.

Boss Watchman climbs up on a chair and shouts:

"Who is it says Newton's Wild Red Raspberry Jelly Factory will be hot as a firecracker on the Fourth of July?"

"We do! We do!" everyone yells.

Hungry Jack helps Suky pass mugs of hot cocoa. Professor Freebee hands over a huge bag of doughnut holes.

Hank's ears are wiggling. "Mike, you'll have to admit my nightmare about the monster was on target. It does have six legs and its color is brown."

"Some monster," I scoff. "A hundred of them wouldn't weigh an ounce."

Hank flips a doughnut hole at me. I catch it between my teeth.

I take out my Super Spy casebook and I write:

"SOLVED, THE CASE OF THE DISAPPEARING SESAME SEEDS."